RESCUE

No Time to Spare

Reading Practice

air	ear	are
air	bear	bare
fair	pear	dare
chair	tear	share
stair	wear	glare
despair	swear	spare

ere	eir
there	their
where	

Contents

Vocabulary:

spare – extra or not needed

glare – a very harsh, bright, dazzling light

steep – with an almost vertical slope

unaware – not conscious of

despair – without hope

dangle – to hang loosely

Cold air tugged at Erin's hair as Danny sped along the street to the lab. "Take care up there!" yelled Danny. Erin grinned. "I need some fresh air! I've had a lot of screen time this week," she said.

Something had been puzzling Erin. Why
had Danny been playing the Space Game

"I forgot my skateboard," shouted Danny

"I was getting it from the porch and I saw
a light inside. I was scared it was a fire."

"I used my spare key to get in. The glare was coming from the screen. I saw you when I sat down. You can spot your hair anywhere."

Erin hugged his hat. "I'm glad I have a spy for a best pal."

They were almost there. The lab was at the top of a steep flight of stairs. Danny stumbled as he ran up the steps. Jack was still safe in his pocket, but Erin was flung into the air!

Chapter 2
Doll Collector

Danny rushed up the stairs to meet Erin's mom. He was unaware that Erin had fallen. "Danny?" said Mom. "Is there a problem? You look scared."

Meanwhile, a little girl spotted Erin as she landed at the bottom of the steps. She bent down and stared at her. "A fairy!" she whispered as she gently picked her up.

Where was Erin? Danny howled with despair as he searched inside his hat. Behind him, a happy little girl was settin off home, with Erin, the fairy, in her pocket

Danny handed Jack to Mom. "We only hav[e] a short window of time for the antidote t[o] work," Mom told Danny. "If we don't fin[d] Erin soon, she will stay that size forever."

"I'll take Jack inside and prepare the antidote," said Mom. "Then I'll help you find Erin. She is smaller than Jack's teddy bear now so she won't have gone a long way."

Polly had raced home with her fairy. She was in her bedroom. "You'll have to share the doll's house with my dolls," said Polly. "It's their house too."

Erin was careful to stay as still as stone. She didn't dare move. Polly gazed down at her. "Now what will you wear?" she asked her fairy.

Polly sat Erin down on a chair from the doll's house. She put a flower in her hair and made her a pair of fairy wings. She gave her a chopped pear to eat.

Chapter 4
Jack Flash!

Back at the lab, Mom was holding a tiny baby Jack in her hand. "Just a big gulp, Jack, and you will be a big boy again," she whispered, as she carefully tipped the antidote into his mouth.

It was not a good taste! Jack glared at Mom. Then, in a flash, he had grown back to his normal size. Mom hugged him tight and then rushed back to join the search for Erin.

Polly had gone to have dinner. This was the time to escape, but it seemed unfair. Polly had cared for Erin. She left her a note outside the doll's house.

Erin dangled a long string from Polly's window and prepared to jump. She didn't even stop to tear off the fairy wings. There was not a second to spare. She had to get back to the lab.